This book belongs to

_____

MICKEY'S ALPHABET SOUP

Published by Advance Publishers
Winter Park, Florida

Written by Wendy Wax   Edited by Bonnie Brook
Penciled by Edwards Artistic Services   Painted by Edwards Artistic Services
Designed by Design Five
Cover art by Peter Emslie
Cover design by Irene Yap

ISBN: 1-885222-76-9
10 9 8 7 6 5 4 3 2

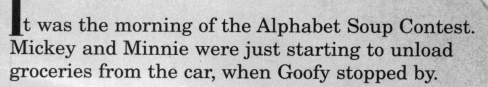

It was the morning of the Alphabet Soup Contest. Mickey and Minnie were just starting to unload groceries from the car, when Goofy stopped by.

"Howdy, pals," said Goofy. "Looks like you bought me some lunch."

"Sorry," said Minnie. "These are ingredients for our secret alphabet soup recipe. It's for the contest."

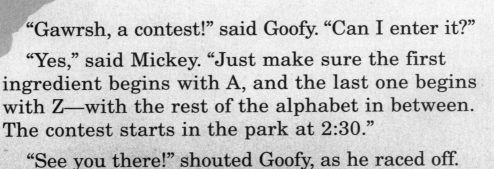

"Gawrsh, a contest!" said Goofy. "Can I enter it?"

"Yes," said Mickey. "Just make sure the first ingredient begins with A, and the last one begins with Z—with the rest of the alphabet in between. The contest starts in the park at 2:30."

"See you there!" shouted Goofy, as he raced off.

After putting the groceries away, Mickey handed Minnie an apron and put one on himself. "Aprons begin with A," he said, "which means we're ready to begin."

Minnie filled a large pot with water while Mickey washed an apple and some asparagus.

Meanwhile, Goofy had just begun to look for a soup pot when he remembered that all his pots were at his aunt's apartment. Instead he filled an old tub with water and aimed a toy airplane toward it. Then he added an arrow and a toy automobile.

"I didn't have breakfast," said Mickey, biting into a banana. Minnie added beets, beans, and berries to the pot on the back burner.

Goofy blew up a balloon, but it burst.

Then he bounced a basketball and batted a baseball.
Both balls landed in the tub, creating lots of bubbles.

7

Mickey cleaned the cauliflower, cabbage, celery, and carrots while Minnie took a picture with her camera.

"This cooking couldn't be more fun," Mickey smiled.

Goofy saw Clarabelle Cow peering through the curtains.

"If you want to taste the best alphabet soup in town, come to the park at 2:30," he said, dropping a cuckoo clock into the soup.

After Clarabelle had left, Goofy added crayons and a castle.

Minnie added dill while Mickey brought up a dozen doughnuts from downstairs.

Then they added eight eggs.

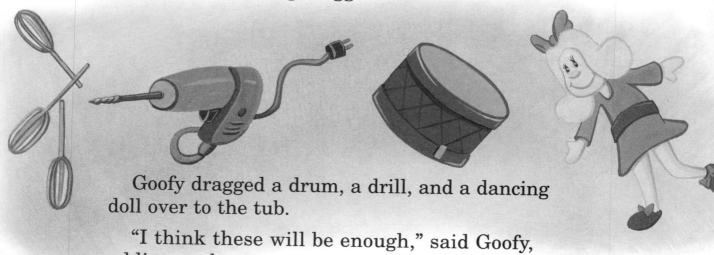

Goofy dragged a drum, a drill, and a dancing doll over to the tub.

"I think these will be enough," said Goofy, adding eggbeaters.

Minnie went out to the front fence to buy figs from Farmer Fritz's truck.

While she was gone, Mickey added French fries.

Goofy fumbled and almost fell into the soup as he added four flowers and five footballs.

"Guess where I got these green peppers," said Mickey.

"From Goofy's garden," Minnie giggled. She gathered a bunch of green grapes and gave one to Mickey.

"It tastes good," said Mickey, grinning.

Goofy gulped down a glass of ginger ale. He grabbed a guitar, a globe, and a gray glove. Then he dropped them into the soup.

"How about some honey?" said Minnie.
"How about a hamburger?" said Mickey.

Goofy wiped his head with a handkerchief as he put a hammer and a hook into the soup.

Ii

Mickey took a carton of ice cream out of the icebox.

"Let's add some pink icing, too," said Minnie.

Into the soup went Goofy's ice skates, iron, and inkwell.

ink

Mickey scooped jelly and jam out of two jars and added them to the soup.

Laughing, Minnie poured in juice from a jug.

"The judges will love this jack-in-the-box," said Goofy. Next he threw in jacks and a jump rope.

Kk

Mickey stirred a kumquat into the soup, while Minnie gave her kitten a kiss.

Goofy added a key and a kite.

Minnie pushed aside a ladder to reach the lettuce while Mickey stirred the soup with a ladle.

Goofy licked a lollipop as he lowered a load of laundry into the soup.

M

"Mind if I add milk, Mickey?" said Minnie, reaching for a measuring cup. There was no answer.

Mickey had marched over to the nearby market to buy some meat and macaroni.

Goofy put on matching mittens and mixed mud,
marbles, and marigolds in the blender.

Nn

"There's nothing like nutmeg," said Minnie.
Next to her, Mickey sprinkled in some nuts.

"Newspapers might be nifty," said Goofy, dropping
them into the soup. He picked up nine nickels and
tossed them in, too.

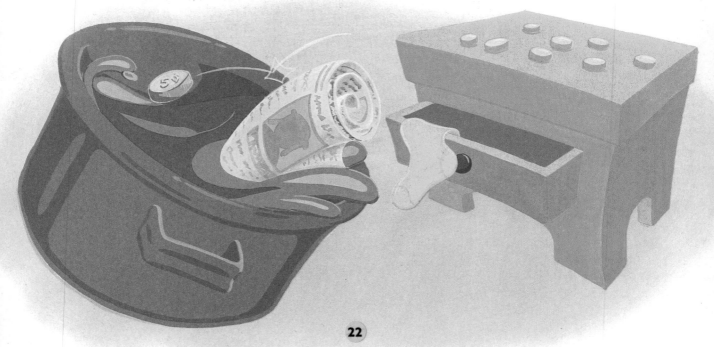

"Oh my," said Minnie. "It's one o'clock. We only have one hour and a half left." She quickly added olive oil and an onion to the soup while Mickey peeled an orange.

Goofy opened the oven and found an oil can and some orchids. Off they went, into the pot. He found an old oar to stir the soup.

Mickey went out on the porch while Minnie picked up a pitcher and poured some punch.

"Perfect," said Mickey, taking a sip. He was getting ready to peel a pound of potatoes.

"We also have popcorn," Mickey said while Pluto fetched some pepper for Minnie.

Goofy poured pebbles, pennies, pillows, Ping-Pong balls, and a purse into the tub.

"How about adding a quart of tomato juice and some quail eggs?" said Mickey.

"Can't quit now," said Goofy, putting some quarters into the tub.

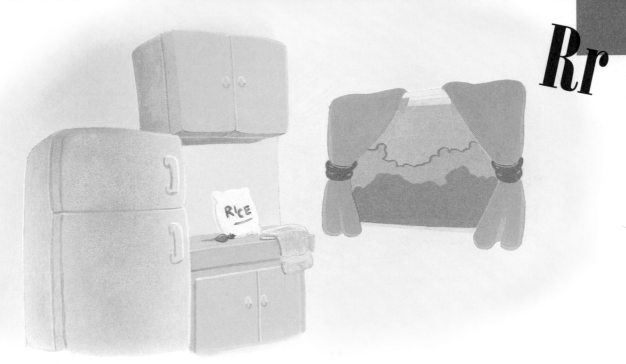

Mickey reached into the refrigerator and pulled out a radish.

"Ready for the rice?" asked Minnie.

Goofy added roses, a roller skate, and a rake to the tub. He had to use a rope to lower a rickety rocking chair in as well.

Minnie shook the salt shaker over the soup. Next she tossed in some sunflower seeds.

Mickey washed and cut the spinach, squash, string beans, and snow peas and slowly added them to the soup.

Goofy put skis and a shovel into the soup as he sang a song.

"Taste this," said Minnie, offering Mickey a teaspoon as she tossed in turnips, tomatoes, and toast.

Goofy unplugged the telephone and threw it into the soup. Then he added toothbrushes, tools, toy tractors, a teepee, and the television.

Uu

"What food begins with U?" Minnie asked Mickey.

"Well," said Mickey. "My uncle gave me something called an ugli fruit last week. It's like an orange."

Goofy tossed an umbrella into his soup.

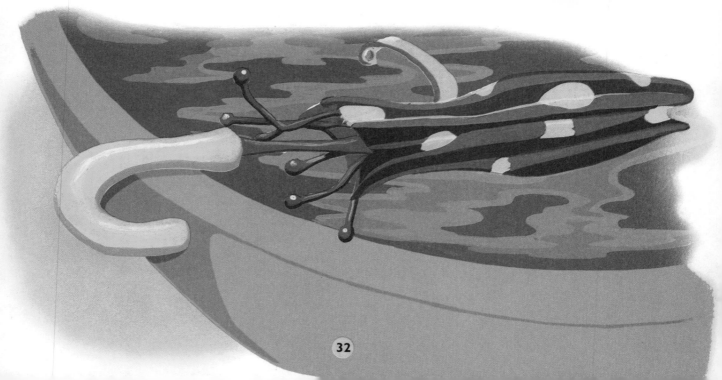

"We've already added lots of vegetables," said Minnie.

"How about adding vanilla or vinegar?" asked Mickey.

Goofy added a violin, a vase, and a vacuum cleaner.

Mickey found some walnuts behind the house. When he went back inside, Minnie weighed them, and put them into the pot. She also added a piece of whole wheat bread and a slice of watermelon.

Outside his window, Goofy
picked up his whistle,
along with a wheel and
a wind-up whale.

"Thank goodness for homemade alphabet cookies," said Mickey. He tossed an X-shaped cookie into the soup.

Minnie added yogurt and a yam.

Goofy threw a xylophone into the soup.

"Yippee!" he yelled as he dropped a ball of yellow yarn and a yo-yo into the tub. "Almost done!"

"Time for the zucchini," said Minnie, tossing it into the pot.

"That means we're done!" said Mickey. "Alphabet Soup Contest, here we come!"

Goofy tossed a zipper into the soup just as his taxi arrived.

As they drove past the zoo, he waved to a zebra.

Minnie, Mickey and Goofy were met by an
excited crowd when they arrived at the park.
By now everyone in town had heard about the
Alphabet Soup Contest. The judges were seated
at a picnic table inside the lodge.

Then Judges Donald and Daisy began to taste all the soups. Finally, they got to Mickey and Minnie's soup.

"Interesting," said Donald, chewing on a piece of popcorn beside the pot.

Daisy was about to taste Goofy's soup when—
"Cuckoo! Cuckoo!" went the cuckoo clock. Daisy's spoon went flying and the crowd laughed.

Finally the judges got together to choose a winner.

"Wait!" said Goofy. "You haven't even tasted my soup."

"Sorry," said Donald. "But footballs, yo-yos, and whatever else you've mixed in there are not things to eat."

A little while later, Daisy announced, "I think there are two winners here." Everyone grew quiet.

"Mickey and Minnie, you've used the tastiest ingredients," said Daisy. "But, Goofy, your ingredients are the most fun to play with!"

"Looks as if we're all winners," said Goofy.

"Yes," said Minnie, "and we had fun too!"